Also by Jean Richardson and Francesca Crespi

The Nutcracker

℘

Text copyright © 1991 by Jean Richardson
Illustrations copyright © 1991 by Francesca Crespi
First U.S. Edition
First published in 1991 by Methuen Children's Books
ISBN 1-55970-142-0
Library of Congress Catalog Card Number 91-55045
Library of Congress Cataloging-in-Publication information is available.

Published in the United States by Arcade Publishing, Inc.,
New York, a Little, Brown company
Typography by Marc Cheshire
1 3 5 7 9 10 8 6 4 2
Printed in Belgium

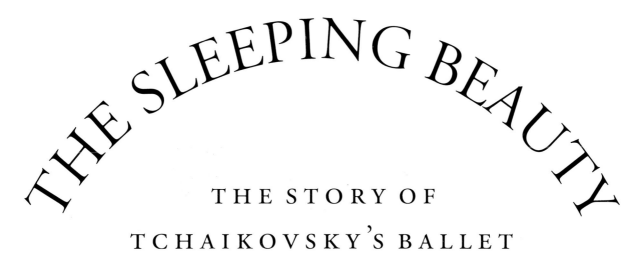

THE SLEEPING BEAUTY

THE STORY OF
TCHAIKOVSKY'S BALLET

RETOLD BY

Jean Richardson

ILLUSTRATED BY

Francesca Crespi

Arcade Publishing ❧ New York

LITTLE, BROWN AND COMPANY

ONCE UPON A TIME there lived a King and Queen who were very unhappy because they had no children.

They took advice from dozens of doctors, drank buckets of water from wishing wells, and tried all kinds of spells. At last, when they had almost given up hope, the Queen gave birth to a daughter.

The King and Queen were overjoyed, and they decided to celebrate by giving little Princess Aurora a magnificent christening.

The King instructed his master of ceremonies, Catalabutte, to invite everyone they had ever known, and the final guest list was yards long.

As the guests began to arrive, Catalabutte looked anxiously down the list for the umpteenth time and prayed that no one had been forgotten.

The baby princess had no fewer than six fairy godmothers. First came the Fairy of the Crystal Fountain, then the Fairy of the Enchanted Garden, followed by the Fairy of the Woodland Glades, the Fairy of the Songbirds, and the Fairy of the Golden Vine. The most important godmother—and the last to arrive—was the Lilac Fairy.

Each in turn danced around Aurora's cradle and presented her with a gift: beauty, wit, the grace of a dancer, the voice of a singer, and the love of music.

But just as the Lilac Fairy was about to present her gift, a clap of thunder announced the arrival of a most unwelcome visitor.

Carabosse was clearly in a mood as black as the fearsome rats who drew her dusky chariot. Why, she demanded furiously, had *she* not been invited to the christening?

Catalabutte, pale and trembling, went down on his knees to apologize—but it was too late.

The wicked fairy was determined to put a curse on the little Princess.

"You will grow up to be very beautiful, my dear," she cackled, "but one day, when you least expect it, you will prick your finger — and die."

As the King tried to comfort the weeping Queen, the Lilac Fairy,
who had yet to give the Princess her gift, spoke.

"Evil cannot be prevented," she said, "but it can be overcome. Princess Aurora will not die but only fall asleep. She and the whole court will sleep for a hundred years, when the spell will be broken by a kiss from a brave and handsome prince."

She looked down at the baby protectively, and everyone breathed a sigh of relief.

But in spite of the Lilac Fairy's promise, the King resolved to take no chances. Every pin, every needle, every spindle that might possibly prick the Princess's finger was banished from the kingdom.

Princess Aurora grew up to be a delightful and beautiful girl. She danced around the palace like a butterfly and loved her parents dearly.

The King and Queen doted on her and gave a splendid party in honor of her coming of age.

Among the many guests were four handsome princes, and Aurora knew that her parents hoped she would fall in love with one of them.

But although she danced with each of them in turn, spinning from one to the other as each offered her a rose, none of them touched her heart.

As she spun away beyond their reach, an old woman stepped forward from the crowd that had gathered around the palace and held out a present. It was a spindle.

Aurora, who had never seen one before and knew nothing of the wicked fairy's curse, was intrigued.

As she examined it, she pricked her finger. It was such a little scratch, such a tiny drop of blood. . . . But when she tried to tell her father that of course she was all right, she felt light-headed, had no strength, just wanted to sleep. . . .

As the King and Queen looked down at their daughter in horror and the sorrowful King ordered her to be carried to their chamber, the old woman who had given Aurora the fatal spindle threw off her disguise. It was Carabosse, the wicked fairy.

But the Lilac Fairy, who was a guest at the party, had not forgotten her promise. With a wave of her wand, the King, Queen, and all the court fell asleep instantly.

As they slept, the hedges and trees twined their branches to form
a leafy green curtain that hid the palace from the rest of the world.

A hundred years later, a handsome prince called Florimund was hunting in a forest not far from the palace. He was in a melancholy mood, and although his friends did their best to amuse him, the Prince sent them away because he wanted to be alone.

He wandered to the shore of a nearby lake and, to his surprise, saw a giant seashell skimming across the water toward him.

He knew it must be an enchanted boat, for it seemed to move by itself. There was only one figure on board, and when it touched the shore, out stepped the Lilac Fairy.

She told Florimund about the spell cast on Princess Aurora and how she could only be awakened by the kiss of a brave and handsome prince.

Florimund didn't know whether to believe her, but when the Lilac Fairy waved her wand, he glimpsed a young girl through the trees. Eager to see more of her, he persuaded the Lilac Fairy to bring the vision closer—and instantly fell in love.

The Prince was now determined to rescue Aurora. He joined the Lilac Fairy in the enchanted boat, and they set off for the palace.

When they arrived, Florimund was amazed to find even the guards asleep.

A cloak of cobwebs covered everything, and the dust rose in clouds as Florimund strode impatiently from room to room.

When he reached the Princess's bedroom, he found her looking even more beautiful than before. He knelt down and gently kissed her.

And when Princess Aurora opened her eyes, she found herself looking at the prince of her dreams.

Now that the spell was broken, the whole court came to life and began to dust and sweep the palace.

The King and Queen were very happy for their daughter to marry
the prince who had rescued them all.

The wedding was the most splendid ever seen in the kingdom,
and Aurora invited all her childhood friends.

There was the White Cat and Puss in Boots, Little Red Riding

Hood and the Wolf, Cinderella and Prince Charming, and, best of all, the Bluebird with his princess.

As the delicate Bluebird darted among the guests, and swooped and soared above them, everyone felt that their dreams would come true.

Princess Aurora and Prince Florimund made a grand entrance to the celebrations and gazed lovingly into each other's eyes as they received a special blessing from the Lilac Fairy.

The young couple, of course, lived happily ever after, and the Lilac Fairy was always welcome at the palace.

But the wicked fairy was never seen again.